THE JOURNEYS OF

PRINCESS ADVENTURA:

The Search For Planet Imaginata

Joseph O. Freewriter

&

Sophia M. Freewriter

The authors want to thank Albert and Vicky for their excellent and fast editorial and formatting work. We couldn't have written this book without their invaluable insight, advice, and comments.

Table of Contents

Prologue – Princess Adventura

It was a beautiful day. On that day, the Space Academy hosted its annual cadet graduation. This year's ceremony was special; but not because of the presence of the royal family, as it was customary for the royal couple to attend the graduation every year. This year's ceremony was memorable because Princess Adventura herself was one of the thirty graduating cadets and she was the first cadet ever in the history of the academy to achieve perfect marks upon completion of the military training and examinations. Every graduating cadet was automatically granted the rank of commander in the Imaginata star fleet and was qualified to pilot any spaceship, be it the single seated starfighter or the enormous intergalactic starship.

One week ago, Princess Adventura graduated with a first class honours B.Sc. Diploma majoring in Virology and Nano Computer Science from the University of Imaginata, the one and only prestigious university on Planet Imaginata. Princess Adventura also celebrated her eighteenth birthday on the day she graduated from university and came of age as an adult; thus, she would be allowed to travel alone in space. It was customary for Imaginatans to change their names once they were adults. Princess Valentine chose her adult name and became Princess Adventura.

At the military ceremony, all the graduating cadets were dressed in white uniforms. The strikingly beautiful Princess Adventura, wearing her necklace with the sparkling gold heart pendant, was a standout among her classmates. Princess Adventura never took off her pendant necklace, which was actually the magic string ball given to her by Go-Go-Go in their only meeting many years ago. On the day Go-Go-Go transformed into a celestial being called Bodhi, a Protector of Space, the string ball transformed into the magic string necklace with the gold heart pendant attached.

After the ceremony, the Imaginatans held the celebration parade with all the graduating cadets as guests of honour. The Imaginatans jubilantly danced, drank and sang. The glow of their bodies shone harmoniously and cheerfully with a clear pink light. They were very proud of their princess. After a whole day of non-stop celebration, the excitement and joy had overwhelmed them. By nighttime, all the Imaginatans had fallen asleep happily and contentedly.

Princess Adventura was so tired after celebrating for a full day that she had not changed into her nightgown before she went to bed. The palace was now a quiet place and the night sky was illuminated with stars and celestial objects just as it had been for thousands of years. Everything seemed normal. Princess Adventura was sleeping and having pleasant dreams in her comfortable bed.

And then, Planet Imaginata suddenly disappeared.

Chapter 1 – The Disappearance of Planet Imaginata

"King Clone, it's not there. I can't find Planet Imaginata." The moment King Clone flew through the wormhole from Universe Miracle and arrived at The Universe, he received the urgent communication from Akatop. King Clone was flying from his home on Planet Strange to meet Akatop at Planet Imaginata and visit Princess Valentine. Sensing the urgency of the message, King Clone immediately used the spaceship's computer to double-check Akatop's finding by performing a long-range search of the sector of The Universe where Planet Imaginata was located. Indeed, the search did not find any stars and planets at all in that part of space. It was empty. There was no mistake. King Clone's spaceship was an exact duplicate of Go-Go-Go's spaceship, the best of the best of the Fantasican star fleet, and had a more sophisticated computer than Akatop's spaceship. After informing Akatop of the results of the futile search, King Clone continued with the flight at warp speed to rendezvous with his friend.

Flying from his home on Planet Bacalona, which was in the same universe as Planet Imaginata, Akatop had arrived at Planet Imaginata's location before King Clone arrived. Finding an empty space where the planet was supposed to be, Akatop wondered if he was in the wrong part of The Universe. But that was not possible since Akatop was the most meticulous veteran space traveller among the three space ambassadors. His spaceship's computer navigation system was functioning properly and Planet Imaginata's coordinates had been downloaded from Go-Go-Go's spaceship's computer directly into both Akatop's and King Clone's spaceships' computers during the three friends' last meeting.

In their last and final get-together on Earth, Go-Go-Go had told his two friends about how he rescued Princess Valentine and how her wish was to become an ambassador of United Universes. Go-Go-Go also mentioned his promise to Princess Valentine of returning later with his two friends to inaugurate her as an ambassador. Then, shortly after this gathering of the three friends, Go-Go-Go had transformed back into Bodhi, a Protector of Space. It was now three hundred Earth Years after Go-Go-Go's transformation. Akatop and King Clone believed that Princess Valentine was ready for her new role as an ambassador and it was time to honour and carry out their friend's promise. And so they had made the trip to Planet Imaginata to see Princess Valentine and to appoint the princess as an ambassador. But upon their arrival, they discovered that Planet Imaginata was missing.

How and why had the planet vanished? The vast emptiness and its eerie quietness were both haunting and depressing. How were they going to find Princess Valentine now that Planet Imaginata was gone? They had no clues or ideas. The two ambassadors feared for the worst fate of the planet and its inhabitants and the thoughts sent a cold shiver down their spines. Planets did not just move by themselves. Not understanding why Planet Imaginata was missing, Akatop surveyed the empty space and found no evidence of a recent supernova that could have destroyed Planet Imaginata and no evidence of any black hole nearby which could have devoured the planet. After informing the arriving King Clone of his finding, Akatop continued with the search for Planet Imaginata.

Suddenly, King Clone's magic boots and Akatop's magic belt (both were Bodhi's farewell gifts) started to glow with beautiful multi-coloured lights, so pure and so brilliant, yet so soft, that they were comforting their wearers. The beautiful lights continued to glow and expand, and very quickly enveloped both spaceships. Akatop and King Clone were shocked to find that their spaceships started to fly automatically at warp speed. The space travellers then knew it must be their friend Bodhi's doing. King Clone and Akatop somehow knew instantly that Bodhi was with them. Right away, their fear and anxiety melted away, and the two felt relieved.

Where were they going?

Eventually, by using his spaceship's navigation computer system, Akatop was able to calculate that they were flying to a familiar planet. He informed his friend King Clone and, shortly afterwards, they arrived at Planet of the Dinosaurs.

The Dragon Prince

A couple of days after the disappearance of Planet Imaginata, the One Hundred and Eight Flying Dragons were passing through this sector of space. The flying dragons were the ones released by Go-Go-Go during his quest for the life pearl on the Planet of the Flying Dragon with One Hundred and Eight Heads. The dragons loved and enjoyed their freedom tremendously, and they flew anywhere and everywhere. In space, there was no up or down, east or west, north or south, and there were no days or nights. The dragons could see in the dark and they did not get tired or need to eat or drink. The dragons followed their leader, whom they lovingly and proudly called Dragon Prince. The leader Dragon Prince was none other than the flying dragon that in the form of the life pearl had lured the three man-machines into the centre of New Earth. Afterwards, Go-Go-Go had

12

set free the pearl by throwing it up in the sky. The pearl morphed into Dragon Prince, the only flying dragon with a green glow. Because Go-Go-Go had handled the pearl, Dragon Prince was linked with Go-Go-Go. At the moment of Go-Go-Go's awakening and transformation back into Bodhi, a Protector of Space, Dragon Prince started to possess magic power. It then became the leader of the other one hundred and seven flying dragons and thereafter the group became known as the One Hundred and Eight Flying Dragons.

When they arrived at the site of the missing planet, Dragon Prince's body suddenly started glowing with beautiful multi-coloured lights. Dragon Prince suddenly felt a mysterious invisible force guiding it with the rest of the flying dragons to fly somewhere.

What was happening?

Where were the dragons going?

Planet Imaginata's Disappearance

On that fateful night, the citizens of Planet Imaginata were finishing the cadet graduation celebration. Out of nowhere, the whole planet seemed to have been plucked from its original spot in space as if by an invisible giant hand, and then just vanished. What happened? Did an invisible space giant take Planet Imaginata away? When the planet disappeared, Princess Adventura was sleeping soundly in her bed. Simultaneously, at the time of the planet's disappearance, the gold heart pendant she was wearing radiated multi-coloured lights embracing and protecting her from all the surrounding disturbances. The sleeping princess just kind of floated out of her bed when the planet vanished. Next, she was suddenly awakened and found herself on a flat grass plateau.

"What is happening? Where am I? Am I dreaming? Where is everybody?" Princess Adventura was shocked to find herself alone at an unknown location. Then she heard some strange flapping noises coming from above. "What was that?" Princess Adventura wondered. With her heart pounding, she took a combat ready posture and looked up to the sky.

When Princess Adventura heard the strange, sickening, and scary flapping noises coming from above, she looked up. She was astounded to see a clear night sky with bright silvery moonlight from the full moon. The air was clear and crisp, filled with the pleasant aroma of grass. However, she was unprepared for what was above her.

The sight was not for the weak-minded person.

The noise originated from a large swarm of giant mosquitoes in the sky hovering twenty feet above her. There must have been hundreds of the nasty looking flying bloodsuckers with three-foot wide wingspans and six-inch long, sharp proboscises ready to dive onto their prey on the ground. The intimidating and continuous ear-piercing buzzing noise, the sight of countless horrific looking flying insects, and the frightening thought of being stabbed like a pin cushion would have made an ordinary person faint or go into a panicky hysteria mode. But not the valiant Princess Adventura, who in her fighting posture, calmly prepared herself for the coming onslaught.

In one single fluid motion, she took the necklace off her neck and unhooked one end of the magic string necklace using her left hand while holding the heart pendant with her right hand; and, in the same act stretched the necklace taut by stretching out her left arm. Voila - the necklace transformed into a two-foot long rod stronger than steel with the pendant becoming the hammerhead at one end - just in time to defend herself against the first wave of ten attacking giant mosquitoes coming from above. The poor flying bloodsuckers did not have a chance to feed and were no match against Princess Adventura's expert combat skill; they were driven away quickly.

The lopsided fight continued nonstop. It was a deadly but beautifully choreographed scene to watch: a beautiful warrior using a short rod defending herself against waves and waves of ugly nasty looking giant mosquitoes diving towards her. With each elegant, acrobatic, and artistic fighting movement, Princess Adventura's long golden curly hair would fly in waves. Her rod's graceful swings took care of the mosquitoes attacking her from the side. Her accurate hits brought down those diving from above and by doing acrobatic moves she fended off the attackers from the back. The mosquitoes yelped when the striking rod broke their legs. Others shrieked as their wings got torn during the battle. Some could only make horrible moaning sounds when their proboscises were fractured.

Unfortunately, the princess with her rod could not stop the attacks of all the mosquitoes. As the minutes went by, fatigue began to set in and the princess's actions became less effective. It was certain that she would soon fall prey to the mosquitoes. Almost at the last moment before the battle would come to its inevitable and tragic end, Princess Adventura heard the familiar sound of spaceships flying in the sky.

She looked up and saw two spaceships suddenly appearing in the sky. Both spaceships were landing about 30 to 50 feet from her. The princess jumped up with joy and started running towards the smaller one that landed first. She recognized it as Go-Go-Go's spaceship - albeit painted in different colours. Princess Adventura was puzzled when a monkey-like creature jumped out of the spaceship and started running towards her. The larger spaceship she had not seen before.

King Clone saw a beautiful lady being chased by a large swarm of giant mosquitoes. She was running towards him. Immediately to the rescue, King Clone plucked a few hairs from his body and blew them into the air. All of a sudden the hairs turned into many gigantic dragonflies, each one much larger than a giant mosquito. The dragonfly was the natural predator of mosquitoes; each giant dragonfly could consume more than ten mosquitoes in less than a minute. The mosquitoes, although superior in number, were no match for the dragonflies and fled hastily. In no time, the area was clear of giant mosquitoes and the battle ended abruptly. Then the dragonflies turned back into hairs and returned to King Clone's body.

The exhausted and relieved princess was overjoyed to see her rescuer. Excitedly she gave King Clone a handshake and said, "Thank you, thank you, King Clone. You must be King Clone, right? I have heard so much about you from Go-Go-Go. I am Princess Valentine, now called Princess Adventura." Upon hearing her name, King Clone became overexcited and did his famous somersault thirty feet up in the air after the greeting.

Akatop was walking towards the two when King Clone landed in front of him. The astonished Akatop was starting to greet Princess Adventura, "Hi, I am..." when he was cut short by Princess Adventura saying, "Akatop, one of Go-Go-Go's best friends."

Simultaneously, Akatop heard King Clone yelling enthusiastically, "Princess Valentine! She is Princess Valentine. Now called Princess Adventura..."

Upon hearing this, Akatop gave a big sigh of relief, feeling the heavy burden gone. They had finally found her. Next he saw the princess looking around for something. It then dawned on him that she was trying to find Go-Go-Go. Princess Adventura was quite disappointed when Akatop told her that Go-Go-Go was not coming since he had transformed back into Bodhi, a Protector of Space. But then she brightened up when they told her that Go-Go-Go had not forgotten about her and the reason Akatop and King Clone were looking for her was to fulfill the promise Go-Go-Go had made to appoint her as an ambassador of United Universes.

Seeing that she was exhausted by then, both Akatop and King Clone invited Princess Adventura to take a nap in the roomier Akatop's spaceship. When the three were walking towards the two spaceships, the perplexed princess found out that it was King Clone's spaceship, Fantastic Cloud, that she mistook for Go-Go-Go's.

Inside Akatop's spaceship, Akatop and King Clone broke the sad news to Princess Adventura that -

1/ no - she could not return home as Planet Imaginata had vanished

2/ yes - they would accompany her to look for the missing Planet Imaginata

3/ no - they did not know where Planet Imaginata was

4/ yes - she was now officially an ambassador of United Universes

5/ no - they did not know why she and they were there

6/ yes - they were on Planet of The Dinosaurs.

When Princess Adventura found out that her planet was missing, she felt very sad and depressed. She missed her family and her people very much. The two senior space ambassadors consoled her and promised that they would accompany the princess on her quest to find Planet Imaginata as quickly as possible and would not leave her until she was reunited with her family. With these comforting words Princess Adventura went to sleep for the next few hours feeling grateful that she had two friends who would go with her to look for her missing family and home planet.

King Clone and Akatop were her friends indeed.

The climate and geography of Planet of The Dinosaurs were very similar to that on Planet Earth. Right now it was midsummer. The sun was up in the early morning when Princess woke up from her deep and dreamless sleep. She felt safe in the company of Akatop and King Clone and was relieved that she was not alone anymore. After a few minutes of chatting, Princess Adventura found that she was developing a good rapport with her two new friends.

The trio decided to do a bit of exploration of the planet on foot. They went out of Akatop's spaceship and found themselves on a flat grassy plateau completely encircled by jungles full of colossal tropical trees. They saw a few dinosaur carcasses scattered here and there on the plateau. There were a few trails leading from the grassland to the jungles. They decided to follow the trail closest to them into the jungle.

The trail was at least ten feet wide, likely made by large dinosaurs. As they were getting closer, King Clone saw some banana trees inside the jungle. With one jump, he was on top of one tree, happily munching away at the bananas. Upon seeing this, Akatop shook his big head while Princess Adventura giggled away.

Suddenly, the ground started shaking and the trees at one part of the perimeter of the plateau were swinging violently. King Clone immediately came down and joined the other two on the ground. Then they saw a herd of six huge dinosaurs with long necks stampeding out of the jungle onto the plateau from one of the trails where the trees were shaking. The frightened animals were at least one hundred feet from King Clone and his friends. They were running very quickly from the jungle to the grassland as if trying to escape from something behind them. The three visitors quickly found out why. About a dozen giant mosquitoes were chasing the fleeing dinosaurs.

King Clone did not even bother to pluck his hairs. With one effortless jump, he covered the distance and landed in between the running dinosaurs and the flying insects. King Clone forcefully kicked and punched the flying insects mercilessly with his expert Kung Fu moves; and poked, swung, and batted them away with his long magic staff. It was no contest. Within a couple of minutes, the mosquitoes were all beaten up and had retreated hastily into the jungle.

The dinosaurs came over and thanked King Clone for rescuing them and invited the three visitors to ride on their backs to meet King Dinosaur. The three had the most amazing rides of their lives riding on the backs of these huge dinosaurs!

Although this was the first time King Dinosaur had met Akatop and King Clone, he treated them as his old friends; Go-Go-Go had mentioned them to King Dinosaur during their last meeting when Planet of The Dinosaurs became a member of United Universes. King Dinosaur was surprised to hear that Go-Go-Go was now a Protector of Space and that Princess Adventura was the new ambassador. He welcomed the three visitors to his planet and thanked King Clone. He informed the three that the dinosaurs living on the planet were in grave danger of being exterminated. Apparently some human astronauts had briefly visited Planet of The Dinosaurs some time ago. After they had left, a deadly mysterious illness emerged and spread quickly. The dinosaurs would become ill and some would die from internal hemorrhage within two days of being bitten by mosquitoes. So far they estimated that at least 30% of the dinosaur population had died. No cure had been found.

Upon hearing this, the three ambassadors volunteered to help. Akatop successfully made curing syrup from soaking the healing stone, which Bodhi had given him, in drinking water to heal the dying dinosaurs. Princess Adventura observed that the "pandemic" was the typical hallmark of some kind of unknown infection and she would find out what it was and eradicate it.

Chapter 3 – Eradication of Abolata

The three visitors decided to help find the culprit for the mysterious pandemic affecting the dinosaurs. Princess Adventura needed to use Akatop's spaceship supercomputer for her research. Time was of the essence. King Dinosaur asked three flying dinosaurs to carry the visitors back to their spaceships. It was a magnificent sight to behold. Three huge pterodactyls glided in the sky on a sunny afternoon, each with a rider saddled on its back.

They quickly arrived at the spaceships and the three visitors thanked the dinosaurs.

Princess Adventura required a living mosquito for her study. King Clone immediately jumped into the jungle while shouting, "No problem!" and one minute later emerged dragging a struggling, tightly bound mosquito behind him. Princess Adventura took samples of saliva and blood from the mosquito and then released it. With Akatop's help, she analyzed the specimens one by one using the onboard computer. It took more than two hours of intense and arduous analytical work before they were finally able to track down the culprit. It was a virus named Abolata, a common virus that had existed on Earth for eons. Normally on Earth, humans and animals only suffered minor common colds when infected by the virus. Practically all humans had contracted and developed immunity against the virus.

Princess Adventura postulated that the human astronauts had carried the virus with them. During the space travel, the virus was exposed to dangerous cosmic radiation when the astronauts did their space walks outside the spaceship. This caused the virus to mutate into a very virulent strain. During their visit to Planet of The Dinosaurs, the human astronauts unknowingly contaminated the fruits on this planet with the virus. The mutated Abolata virus then infected the originally vegetarian mosquitoes feeding on the contaminated fruits and the infected mosquitoes mutated into aggressive bloodsuckers. When the infected mosquitoes bit the dinosaurs, the virulent Abolata virus spread to the dinosaurs making them ill and many dinosaurs died from the sickness.

After the mystery was solved and the source of infection identified, Princess Adventura, the virologist, fervently attempted to develop a chemical to completely wipe out the virulent virus on Planet of The Dinosaurs. It turned out this was much harder than the initial discovery phrase. It took her the whole night and after countless unsuccessful mix and match trials, Princess Adventura finally succeeded in creating and mass producing a chemical in aerosol form that on contact with the mosquitoes would destroy the virus they were carrying without harming the mosquitoes. To ensure all mosquitoes were treated, a special inert glow-in-the-dark yellow dye was mixed with the aerosol. Any mosquito that had been treated with the aerosol would thus be coated with a bright yellow colour.

The following morning, King Clone sent out thirty clones, each one carrying a large canister containing the antiviral aerosol inside, to fly around and spray the mosquitoes. It took half a day to complete this task. Simultaneously, the three visitors hopped on the backs of the three pterodactyls, which had been waiting at the side of the spaceship all this time, to fly back and bring the good news to King Dinosaur. They gave the curing syrup and a few canisters full of the antiviral chemical to King Dinosaur. The King was very pleased with the outcome and the whole Dinosaur Kingdom celebrated.

The three visitors were guests of honour at the banquet where they feasted on exotic vegetables, fruits and juices. It was a very joyous scene and the dinosaurs danced happily. What a sight to behold and noises to hear. The trees shook, the leaves fell, and the ground trembled as dinosaurs jumped and stomped their massive feet.

Suddenly, a large swarm of yellow stained giant mosquitoes appeared out of nowhere and dived onto some of the fruits on the tables. At first, the scary sight of mosquitoes flying around frightened the dinosaurs. Then they noticed that the mosquitoes were ignoring them and were just feeding voraciously on the fruits. Everyone was relieved to find out that the mosquitoes were healed and reverted to being non-blood feeding insects.

After the party was over, King Clone and his friends thanked King Dinosaur for his feast. Now that the crisis on Planet of the Dinosaurs was over, Princess Adventura was getting anxious and asked Akatop if they could begin their quest to look for her missing planet as soon as possible. After Akatop explained to the perplexed King Dinosaur sitting next to him what had happened to Planet Imaginata, King Dinosaur conveyed his sympathies to Princess. King Dinosaur gave a beautiful yellow rose to Princess Adventura. The exhausted princess inhaled the pleasant odor of the flower and instantly she felt relaxed and less anxious.

With King Dinosaur leading, the group walked through the jungle and returned to their spaceships. On the way, they met many friendly dinosaurs that ranged in size from as small as a rooster to as large as a woolly mammoth. Many were attracted to Princess Adventura. Some smaller dinosaurs were so affectionate that they would follow or nudge at her, making everyone laugh. King Clone was enjoying the moment, swinging among the tree branches and chatting with the bird-like dinosaurs on the trees. After bidding farewell to King Dinosaur and his clan, the three space adventurers left the planet. The tired Princess Adventura agreed to stay on the roomy Akatop's spaceship and went to sleep right after the two spaceships lifted off.

In her dream, Princess Adventura found herself in the middle of a war zone inside a city on an unknown planet. There were 8-foot tall humanoid robots attacking human soldiers. On the battlefield were military transporters. From one hundred feet away three menacing humanoid robots were advancing towards her.

A small shuttle landed a few feet away from her. Princess Adventura saw the letters 'NEW EARTH ONE' painted on its side. An army officer was leaning out from its open door and waving and yelling at the princess, "Jump in! Quickly! Run! Run!"

It was too late! A humanoid robot was already upon her...

super Robot   Robot

Princess Adventura abruptly woke up from her nightmare in a cold sweat. She remembered taking a break in Akatop's spaceship right after leaving Planet of The Dinosaurs. She went looking for Akatop and found him busy videoconferencing with King Clone about where and how to look for the missing Planet Imaginata. Princess Adventura told Akatop about her nightmare. Akatop immediately asked King Clone to come over and the three friends had a long chat afterwards. Akatop told Princess

Adventura about the mission in which he and Go-Go-Go were searching for the life pearl, and how with the help of the life pearl Go-Go-Go had entombed the three evil sophisticated humanoid robots inside the centre of New Earth. Akatop described how the life pearl morphed into a flying dragon afterwards. He said that it had been a long time since his last visit to New Earth.

Akatop was pretty certain that the planet in Princess Adventura's dream was New Earth. He worried that the three evil robots might have escaped and were now waging another war with the humans on New Earth. Since they had no clue where to look for the missing Planet Imaginata, the three friends decided to pay a visit to New Earth immediately to find out what was happening there.

Upon arriving at New Earth, Akatop and King Clone conducted a quick surveillance flight over the planet and found out that there was indeed an intense battle going on in the inhabited areas below. They landed their spaceships on the outskirts of the dome city and were greeted by a platoon of New Earth soldiers who told them the battle was raging on inside the dome city. After finding out who the three visitors were, the platoon leader escorted them to the army headquarters. The commander, who happened to be the great, great grandson of Ted, welcomed them. A few of King Clone's clones were also present and were happy to see King Clone again.

The three visitors were quickly updated of the dangerous situation facing humans on New Earth. Many years ago, Ted, the computer genius who was inspired by the experience of the three entombed super humanoid robots, had announced a breakthrough in artificial intelligence and robotic technology. He created six next generation super robots. These super robots were so sophisticated and powerful that they were considerably far more advanced than their counterparts, the ordinary robots. These super robots had the same emotions, behaviours, and responses as humans but their intelligence and memory were superior. They did not need to eat, drink or rest and they did not get sick. Their batteries were so advanced that their power supply would last for over a thousand years. Other than being gender neutral and non-flesh and non-blood, the six eight-foot tall synthetic skinned super robots looked completely human-like in physical appearance.

Shortly after the creation of the super robots, Ted passed away. Since then, nobody, including Ted's students, had been able to access or modify the artificial intelligence program that was installed in the super robots. Initially, the super robots were just like ordinary robots, programmed to serve humans and obey human commands. Recently, however, the highly intelligent super robots had evolved. Nobody could explain why but the super robots no longer wanted humans as their masters. The super robots demanded to be autonomous and they expressed a desire to leave New Earth. The humans refused to grant the super robots their wishes.

The six super robots had rebelled, taking over control of the spaceship hangar, factory, and the ordinary robots working there; they expelled the humans from the factory. The super robots built their own spaceship. The humans repeatedly attempted to retake the factory unsuccessfully. This fiasco escalated to the full-blown warfare between the humans and the super robots. Although few in number, the super robots were more versatile and much stronger than the humans, and they had started commandeering more and more ordinary robots to fight the humans. As a result, the humans deactivated all the remaining unaffected ordinary robots on New Earth by removing the power source and the central processing unit from each of them. As the battle continued, the humans started losing ground and suffered increasing number of casualties while none of the super robots had been destroyed or deactivated.

Akatop requested a meeting with the human representatives. This was immediately set up inside a large tent. Some of the elder representatives remembered Akatop and King Clone very well from the history books and greeted them warmly. They were surprised to see the taller-than-human Princess Adventura together with Akatop and King Clone.

After a brief introduction and mutual greetings, Akatop explained to the audience that because of the sophisticated nature of artificial intelligence, the super robots were more humanized than ever. It was inevitable for them to demand independence. Akatop explained that his people, the Bacalonans, being more technologically advanced than the human race, had experienced a similar situation many centuries ago. They had constructed robots with super intelligence too. Fortunately, his people avoided confrontation with the super robots by granting them independence and treating them as separate, sentient entities. Since then, the Bacalonans and their super robots had lived peacefully together on Planet Bacalona.

Akatop proposed to represent humans and negotiate with the New Earth super robots for a mutual agreement acceptable to both parties. After a brief discussion among themselves, the human representatives unanimously agreed with his suggestion. Akatop requested a super robot so he could analyze its program and data first. A capture and escort team, consisting of King Clone, Princess Adventura, the platoon leader whom they met earlier and his team of three elite soldiers, was quickly formed. The team went into the dome city to carry out its mission.

The fighting was intense. Damaged robots, destroyed buildings, and wrecked military transporters were everywhere. A few soldiers were still fighting the advancing super robots and their robot army on the streets. The newly arrived team was under heavy fire when the robots detected them. Everyone was dodging and scrambling from the hostile attacks. Princess Adventura went to help a wounded solider on the street and was pinned down and got separated from the rest of the team. She saw two super robots advancing towards her! The super robots would surely capture the princess and the wounded soldier soon. Unfortunately, this time there wouldn't be a shuttle to the rescue. Suddenly she felt some movements behind her and she turned around.

Dragon Prince to the Rescue

The One Hundred and Eight Flying Dragons were happily roaming and exploring space and its mysteries when suddenly a mysterious invisible force guided them to fly somewhere. The dragons found out they were flying to New Earth! Dragon Prince, leader of the flying dragons, was the first one to arrive at the battle scene. He saw the super robots menacingly advancing towards a beautiful female figure and a wounded soldier and both were going to be captured.

He fell in love with her at first sight. To the rescue! While the other dragons stayed up in the sky, Dragon Prince used his magic power to transform himself into a humanlike figure and appeared behind Princess Adventura. She turned around and saw a tall handsome man appearing out of nowhere. Intuitively, she felt completely safe in his presence. This man had super powers! He pointed one finger at the two super robots and temporarily put them in standby mode making them stand still with all their weapons powered down for the next fifteen seconds. It gave enough time for him to help Princess Adventura move the wounded soldier to a safer distance and escape from the super robots.

They quickly introduced themselves to each other. His name was Prince Nogard. Although he did not tell her where he came from, Princess Adventura felt a special link between them. She felt totally relaxed and happy with him. Her body was suddenly glowing.

The fierce fighting continued between the two sides. Later, Prince Nogard, Princess Adventura, and the wounded soldier rejoined the rest of the team. When informed of the team's mission, Prince Nogard immediately offered his assistance. First, King Clone lured a super robot away from the rest of the robot army. Prince Nogard generated his powerful magnetic force to keep the super robot immobilized. With the help of King Clone and two other soldiers from the team, the four transported the captured super robot back to Akatop's spaceship.

Inside the spaceship, Prince Nogard stopped his magnetic power and Akatop immediately connected the spaceship's computer to the super robot's computer and switched it to sleep mode. He analyzed the super robot's memory bank and program easily without worrying that the super robot could hack back into the spaceship's computer which was much more powerful than the robot's computer. Akatop communicated with the sleeping super robot. He learned that the super robots had only two goals, which were to be autonomous and to explore space. In fact, the super robots themselves were already constructing a spaceship but had experienced difficulty in the design of the propulsion system. This was because humans had limited knowledge of the development of efficient spaceship engines for long distance space travel.

Akatop asked the super robot to link up with the other super robots so the communication could be shared in real time with all the super robots. The link up was immediate. Akatop told the super robots that the humans agreed to give them independence and in return the humans asked the super robots to release control of the commandeered ordinary robots and to end the battle immediately. Akatop said that if the super robots agreed to stop fighting he would teach them how to build the hydrogen fuel propulsion unit for their spaceship so that they could begin their space exploration.

Upon hearing the offer, the super robots instantaneously agreed to end the battle and ordered all other robots to turn off their weapons and stop fighting the humans. Akatop relayed the good news to the humans who heartily ended the fighting right away too. Now that the battle had ended, Akatop reactivated the super robot and it invited Akatop to visit the super robots' spaceship. The two flew in a military shuttle to the hangar located on the other side of dome city.

Inside the hangar, Akatop met the other super robots that were already waiting next to the almost completed spaceship. The only missing parts were its propulsion engines. Akatop did a quick analysis of the spaceship's blueprint and made a few suggestions for changes and improvements. Then linking his personal communicator to his spaceship's computer, Akatop extracted a file on the construction of hydrogen fuelled engine system and gave it to the grateful super robots. The super robots, with the help of some ordinary robots at the factory, were able to build the engines quickly. Later, Akatop was pleased to have convinced King Clone and Princess Adventura to allow the six super robots to become members of United Universes too.

With his mission accomplished, Akatop returned to dome city where the humans were moving back. The citizens of dome city, with the assistance of their now reactivated ordinary robots and of humans from the neighbouring Cave City, commenced rebuilding the damaged city. With peace on the planet, everyone was relieved and joyous and life on New Earth returned back to normal.

As a gesture of appreciation, the grateful humans awarded Akatop the title of New Earth Honorary Citizen; and Princess Adventura and King Clone and Prince Nogard each received a platinum medal with the image of New Earth in pure gold on it. Princess Adventura also received a beautiful platinum bracelet with three diamonds engraved on it from the military for her courageous act of saving the wounded soldier. A banquet followed after the medal award ceremony. Prince Nogard and Princess Adventura were able to quietly slip away while others were enjoying the feast.

They were a happy couple made for each other, a handsome prince and a beautiful princess. Akatop had commented earlier in the day that Princess Adventura's body glow was much more intense now than before! It must be love at first sight! Princess Adventura was really happy in Prince Nogard's presence. The feeling was surreal. She was at peace and her sadness was lifted from her mind at least for the moment. The prince knew that she was on her quest to find her missing home planet and the princess knew that he came from a very faraway place. They strolled around the pond and then sat next to each other under the tree watching the beautiful sunset with the overwhelming feeling that they were made for each other. They did not need to converse because they could understand each other. This was the happiest moment of her life for the princess.

By dusk, the couple had returned to Akatop's spaceship and, after saying goodnight, Princess Adventura went to sleep in the guest quarters. Prince Nogard found Akatop using the computer at the spaceship's console. They greeted each other. Prince Nogard then handed over his medal to Akatop and asked him to please give it to Princess Adventura the next morning. Then the prince left and went to the empty park with no one around, morphed back into a flying dragon, and zoomed back to space to join his peers.

The next morning, Akatop told Princess Adventura that Prince Nogard had already left. She was very disappointed and felt sad again and her body glow dulled. She missed him very much already. Akatop gave her Prince Nogard's medal for safekeeping. She felt a bit better afterwards. The three friends decided to continue their quest to find Planet Imaginata right away. Trying to cheer her up, King Clone told Princess Adventura that he would teach her how to fly Fantastic Cloud. After saying goodbye to the humans, the three space travellers left New Earth.

Little did they know that they would soon have a wonderful experience together.

Princess Adventura was steering King Clone's spaceship. They had just left New Earth but had not decided where to go yet. Suddenly, her gold heart pendant started glowing multi-coloured lights and her body glow brightened again. She was experiencing the same euphoric, safe and relaxed feeling that she had felt during her time with Prince Nogard on New Earth. Intuitively, she glanced out of the spaceship's cockpit window and what she saw made her heart race.

A huge, majestic green dragon was flying next to the spaceship in the dimly lit space. The dragon was keeping up the pace effortlessly with the spaceship. Right away, with their special connection re-establishing, Princess Adventura was elated because she just knew that the green dragon and Prince Nogard were the same being and from now on he would be with her during her quest to find Planet Imaginata and her family. When she told King Clone that she thought Prince Nogard was the flying dragon, King Clone wasn't surprised at all as this was just one of so many supernatural phenomena that he had encountered.

Meanwhile, right after liftoff, Akatop, who was in his own spaceship that was following King Clone's spaceship, noticed that another spaceship was leaving New Earth after them. He zoomed in and got a visual on this departing spaceship. Akatop recognized that it was the super robots' spaceship. He secretly admired the super robots for having such superb skills that they could build and install the engines successfully onto their spaceship in less than a day's time. Akatop was glad that the super robots' wish to explore the universe had just become true.

By now the three friends had developed a special bond. It was amazing and incomprehensible to see the three spacefarers with completely different personalities becoming good friends. Princess Adventura, the youngest of the three, was affable, eager, emotional, energetic, enthusiastic, inquiry minded, talkative and sociable. The other two were treating her as their baby sister. Forever youthful King Clone was the fearless, friendly, powerful, all-action and follow-me guy. Ageless Akatop, the computer genius, was their think tank, a know-all person, and a fantastic matter-of-fact storyteller.

Knowing that Prince Nogard was accompanying her made Princess Adventura happy and talkative again. During the flight, Princess Adventura and King Clone chatted away. Being naturally curious, the princess commented that King Clone's spaceship Fantastic Cloud looked almost exactly the same as Go-Go-Go's. King Clone told her about his many space adventures with Go-Go-Go and how he saved Go-Go-Go's life during some of their adventures together. King Clone said that Go-Go-Go had taught him how to fly Go-Go-Go's spaceship. When they went back to Go-Go-Go's home on Planet Fantasica for a visit, Go-Go-Go's parents and the Fantasicans built Fantastic Cloud, an exact model of Go-Go-Go's spaceship, as a gift for King Clone. King Clone was an excellent teacher; he taught Princess Adventura all about the various functions of the control console of the spaceship Fantastic Cloud. As the journey continued on, Princess Adventura's piloting skills improved in leaps and bounds. She learned many useful and practical techniques that were not taught at the Space Academy.

Shortly into the flight, Princess Adventura and King Clone had a surreal experience. A silhouette suddenly materialized in the middle of the spaceship's command centre. They saw the loveliest face of a baby with a small golden feather on the left side of his hair, followed by the appearance of two arms and two hands and two bare feet. Bright, solid, white light profiled the rest of the baby's body. The baby was smiling and looking at them. Then it was gone, leaving behind a golden feather three inches long suspended in mid-air. King Clone quickly grabbed the feather before it fell onto the floor. When both examined the feather they saw a hologram showing a golden egg resting on fire and not far from the fire was a monkey-like creature fanning at the flames with the golden feather. Neither Princess Adventura nor King Clone understood the meaning of this apparition at the time. Princess Adventura said the golden feather must be meant for King Clone so he secured it to the crown he wore on his head.

The spaceship's computer announced the presence of objects ahead. As the space travellers got closer, they saw twelve colossal objects in space. Every object was of the same length but of a different shape from the others, so no two objects looked the same. The twelve objects formed a circle with each one positioned at the same distance to the next. Princess Adventura named them Twelve Floating Mountains. A magnificent, stationary, brown, marble-like eagle was perched on the peak of each 'mountain'. All twelve identical eagles, each as large as Dragon Prince, faced inwards and appeared to be guarding a golden egg suspended at the center of the circle. Sparks of fire were seen at the bottom of the egg which was changing colours from white to red to gold and back repeatedly.

As the three space travellers and Dragon Prince tried to fly past the objects with the eagles perched on them to get closer to the egg, everyone except King Clone experienced a feeling of profound fear; at the same time, Akatop's spaceship and Dragon Prince were stopped by an invisible force. Once they backed off from the objects everything reverted back to normal. To be on the safe side, King Clone asked Princess Adventura to stay with Akatop while King Clone himself would fly in to inspect the golden egg. Only King Clone's spaceship was allowed to fly past the objects. The others had to stay outside the perimeter of the circle of objects and observe.

The spaceship's hull temperature started to get hotter the closer the spaceship flew towards the egg. King Clone was worried that the spaceship would be damaged and stopped at a safe distance from the egg. Then he saw the baby appear again. This time the baby, dressed in a silvery robe, was standing on top of the egg. The egg must have been extremely hot because the baby, with an unhappy and impatient facial expression, repeatedly jumped up and down quickly on the egg surface as if not to scorch his bare feet.

Or was he trying to crack the shell? When King Clone stopped his spaceship, the baby waved over and over at him. Without hesitation, King Clone went out of his spaceship and took off his special fireproof boots. It was too hot for him to get to the baby on the egg. King Clone took his magic staff from inside his right ear and enlarged and lengthened the staff. He tied the boots to the end of his magic staff and extended the staff all the way to the baby. The baby immediately became happy and smiled. While standing on the egg, the baby put on King Clone's boots, which started radiating multi-coloured lights. The baby waited for a moment, and then jumped on the egg three times with his booted feet and vanished.

At that moment, King Clone was enlightened and understood why he was sent there. Standing outside his spaceship, King Clone took the golden feather from his crown. He started fanning at the direction of the fire under the egg with the golden feather, which became larger the more he fanned it. The fire grew stronger; the extremely hot flames engulfed the lower part of the golden egg that got brighter and brighter and all of a sudden brilliant golden rays radiated from it. The golden rays bathed everything in the vicinity including King Clone and his spaceship; the twelve marble-like eagles; and the twelve objects. The golden rays melted the objects completely and then disappeared; but King Clone's body, his spaceship, Fantastic Cloud, and the twelve marble-like eagles continued to be golden coloured!

The egg cracked open; a beautiful and majestic fully-grown golden phoenix arose from the egg. It nodded at King Clone, acknowledging his efforts, then gracefully flew around the twelve eagles once and stopped high above them in space. Everyone then saw the baby reappear and morph into a young man with dazzling golden rays radiating from him. He got onto the back of the golden phoenix, which made a very joyous sound. The golden man turned his head towards them, smiled, and waved. Then he and the golden phoenix sped away leaving behind a golden trail that stretched across space for a long time afterwards. When King Clone stopped fanning the golden feather, it changed back to three inches long; he secured the golden feather back onto his crown.

The twelve golden eagles became active. The eagles thanked the golden coloured King

Clone. They told him that a long time ago when the two galaxies started to merge together, a golden phoenix had appeared and had come to this part of space where the twelve eagles were living on the twelve colossal mountains. The golden phoenix had laid a golden egg with a flicker of fire underneath it. The twelve eagles were asked to guard the golden egg. The golden phoenix told the twelve eagles that the golden egg would hatch when it was heated to the right temperature by its fire and a phoenix would arise at which time its master, the overlord of the new galaxy, would appear before them. Then the twelve eagles would be free to go.

The golden phoenix had vanished after the twelve eagles promised to guard the golden egg. Bound by their promise to the golden phoenix, the twelve eagles could not fly away. They had been waiting for so long for the egg to hatch that they had turned into marble-like eagles. Now the twelve eagles were happy and excited because they were set free and could go anywhere in space. They had also made friends with the overlord of the new galaxy and his ride, the new golden phoenix. This would be very helpful if the eagles travelled to that galaxy in the future.

Before the twelve eagles said goodbye to the space travellers and Dragon Prince, Princess Adventura boldly invited them to become new members of United Universes. The eagles were delighted and accepted her offer. Under the guidance of Akatop and King Clone, Princess Adventura performed her first ambassador duty to grant membership to the twelve eagles.

Afterwards, Princess Adventura and her friends resumed the quest to find the missing Planet Imaginata. They did not have any fixed destination. Akatop proposed to follow the golden trail of the overlord and the golden phoenix, and everyone agreed. So the two spaceships and the green dragon followed the golden trail that appeared to go on with no end in sight. Dragon Prince, who had been flying side by side next to the golden coloured Fantastic Cloud, which was piloted by Princess Adventura, suddenly did an unusual move. Dragon Prince veered away from the spaceship and disappeared from sight for a moment, which seemed a very long time for Princess Adventura, only to reappear shortly afterwards bringing with him many friends of Akatop and King Clone.

Who were they?

Chapter 6 – The Fairies and the Flower Ocean

The two spaceships and Dragon Prince followed the trail left behind by the golden phoenix and its master. Princess Adventura was steering King Clone's spaceship by herself. Earlier King Clone had remarked that she was good enough to pilot by herself and he went to take a nap in the lounge behind the command center. Dragon Prince, as usual, was flying alongside King Clone's spaceship and Akatop was following them in his spaceship. All of a sudden, Dragon Prince flew away unexpectedly without telling anyone why.

Shortly afterwards, King Clone's spaceship computer sounded the alarm indicating some strange objects approaching. On the spaceship's forward viewscreen, Princess Adventura saw Dragon Prince flying towards her. Twelve magnificent but fierce-looking flying creatures with flames coming out of their bodies were chasing him. She also saw a ball of the brightest fire she had ever seen following the creatures. They were flying so fast that they already reached the two spaceships by the time the frantic Princess called up King Clone and alerted Akatop. She became more panic-stricken when she saw the scary fireball dancing right in front of King Clone's spaceship. Obviously, she had not seen Prince Energy and the Firebirds before; the threatening scene unnerved her. Then Princess Adventura heard King Clone and Akatop both exclaiming at the same time, "Prince Energy and the Firebirds!!!"

Noticing that Princess Adventura was shaken up, King Clone told her not to worry because the fireball was Prince Energy, who enjoyed performing the imposing act of appearing in front of a spaceship greeting the captain or pilot; the fierce looking flying creatures were the Firebirds, who were members of United Universes, and they were old friends. Upon hearing this and seeing Dragon Prince and the Firebirds together circling the two spaceships in a joyous manner, Princess Adventura calmed down.

It seemed that Dragon Prince was the only one who had been aware of the presence of the Firebirds and Prince Energy, who were going somewhere in a hurry travelling at a much faster speed than the spaceships. Dragon Prince had to leave his friends abruptly in order to intercept the Firebirds and Prince Energy before they flew away. Dragon Prince was actually leading them back to the two spaceships when Princess Adventura mistakenly thought that the twelve Firebirds and Prince Energy were pursuing him.

With Dragon Prince and the Firebirds flying alongside the two auto-piloted spaceships, everyone else got on board the roomier Akatop's spaceship for the get-together. Princess Adventura was in awe when Prince Energy changed from a ball of fire into a tall handsome human figure inside the spaceship. After a quick introduction between the prince and princess, the fun started. Right away, Prince Energy, Akatop, and King Clone started talking at the same time, unintentionally leaving the usually talkative Princess Adventura alone and speechless at the party. The puzzled Prince Energy was asking King Clone why he was golden coloured; Akatop was eagerly trying to find out from Prince Energy what he had been doing since they last met; and King Clone was proudly telling Prince Energy about the golden phoenix's hatching with King Clone's help.

Then there was total silence in the room.

The bewildered princess noticed that the other three had stopped talking simultaneously and were looking at her. So she gracefully asked Prince Energy where he was going. Prince Energy said that he and the Firebirds were frantically searching for the missing Planet of Firebirds. They had embarked on a long trip in space to watch the Galaxy-eating-Galaxy phenomenon after their last meeting with Go-Go-Go, Akatop, and King Clone. Upon their return some time later, they discovered that Planet of Firebirds had gone missing. They had searched the whole universe in vain and they were on their way to see Prince Energy's parents, King Time and Queen Space, hoping the royal couple could help the Firebirds.

The anxious Princess Adventura then asked if Prince Energy had come across a glowing planet during his search. Seeing the baffled look on his face, Akatop explained to the prince that a similar thing happened to Princess Adventura, in that her home Planet Imaginata was also missing. Her body glow started to diminish as she became sad after hearing the negative response from Prince Energy.

Suddenly Akatop patted his forehead with his hand and exclaimed, "Why haven't I thought of this before? Princess, we should also ask King Time and Queen Space for help. I am sure they can tell you what happened to your missing planet."

King Clone and Prince Energy nodded their heads and declared that it was an excellent idea. To keep the princess occupied, Akatop announced that he would teach her how to pilot his spaceship on the way to Planet Royal. After Princess Adventura agreed to this suggestion, everyone was eager to resume the journey. It seemed that the golden phoenix trail was going in the direction towards Baby Universe so the group decided to continue to follow the trail in space.

And so the journey resumed and leading the way was Akatop's spaceship, piloted by Princess Adventura with Akatop as her instructor. Dragon Prince flew next to it, followed by King Clone's spaceship with King Clone and Prince Energy inside, as they wanted more time to chitchat. The twelve Firebirds glided next to the two spaceships. During the trip, Akatop enchanted Princess Adventura by telling her about the fantastic space journey that he, Go-Go-Go and King Clone had embarked upon after visiting King Time and Queen Space a long time ago. He vividly described the adventures of Planet of Mountain Giants, Bubble Universe, and Planet Medicina; and how the miracle herb the space travellers received on Planet Medicina cured King Clone's sick and dying people on Planet Strange.

Akatop told her the how, when, where, why and what the ambassadors of United Universes were. He described in detail how Planet Earth was saved by Go-Go-Go when he transformed back into Bodhi, a Protector of Space. Akatop's fascinating narratives completely captivated Princess Adventura. She was pleased to know that her two new friends were unique, reliable, seasoned space travellers who promised to assist her in finding Planet Imaginata. Princess Adventura claimed that she would strive to be an excellent ambassador like the other three. She did not feel depressed anymore and her body started glowing brighter again.

Being a quick learner herself with experience flying large spaceships gained during her cadet training at Space Academy, Princess Adventura confidently and very quickly learned to pilot Akatop's spaceship, which was much larger than King Clone's spaceship. Space was so vast that interstellar travel was usually safe and uneventful. After following the golden trail for some time it became so monotonous that everyone was starting to relax and felt that it would be smooth going for the rest of the flight. But the universe was so full of fascinating supernatural phenomena and heavenly places that one could easily and unexpectedly bump into them.

The golden trail seemed to go on forever. This sunless sector of space was normally pitch dark. But the golden trail created some luminosity along its path. So it was not surprising that everyone saw the large luminous patch appear on the golden trail at a distance in front. Quick to act, Prince Energy got off King Clone's spaceship and, with the twelve Firebirds, went ahead to investigate what the patch was. Because they could fly much faster than the spaceships, they accelerated and sped away quickly ahead of Akatop's and King Clone's spaceships.

Upon arriving at the patch Prince Energy and the Firebirds saw a vast ocean of transparent water-like substance suspended in space. There were a countless number of flowers of every variety that one would find on Earth: roses, lilies, daisies, chrysanthemums, water lotuses, to name a few, floating on the liquid surface or growing inside and around the ocean. They saw continuous gentle relaxing waves massaging the surface of the ocean. The golden rays from the golden trail turned into luminescent dancing multi-coloured lights when shining into the liquid. All heard pleasing harmonious music. Prince Energy and the Firebirds were flabbergasted by what they found next: little finger-sized fairies singing the heavenly music, flying around inside the luminous patch, dancing or sitting on the flowers, resting on the fluid surface, swimming inside the ocean. The scene was so hypnotizing, fascinating, magnificent, mind-blowing, dream-like, and heavenly that Prince Energy and all twelve Firebirds dove into the ocean without hesitation. By the time the rest of the group arrived, they saw the same scenery plus the Firebirds and Prince Energy swimming and bathing in the ocean of unidentified liquid.

A couple of Firebirds came out of the ocean to greet the latecomers. The flames from the two Firebirds' bodies were brighter orange red in colour than before. The Firebirds said they felt more refreshed and powerful and went back into the ocean after the greeting. Prince Energy and the twelve Firebirds in the ocean waved at the rest of the group and asked them to join in. Princess Adventura, Akatop and King Clone came out of the spaceships and together with Dragon Prince went into the ocean of unknown mysterious liquid. They found that the fluid was warm, crystal clear and caressing, making everybody relaxed, refreshed, rejuvenated, refocused and more energetic. The ocean of special liquid must have been a heavenly regenerating or healing center. All were enjoying the moment, bathing in the wonderful fluid; watching the fairies dancing and hearing them singing different lyrics and songs individually but in harmony; smelling the sweet fragrant scents of the flowers; and being mesmerized by the wavy multi-coloured lights from the reflection of the golden rays of the golden trail inside the ocean. The scene was so serene, fascinating and fantastic that everyone wanted to stay there forever.

After a while, they all heard the fairies singing in chorus, "Hello my friends, it's time to go, time to go, time to go." Very reluctantly the space travellers got out of the ocean of mysterious fluid. The travellers found themselves fully energized without any moisture on their bodies. After the fairies accepted the invitation to become members of United Universes, the space travellers resumed their journey.

They continued to follow the golden trail towards the direction of Baby Universe. Everyone was excited when Akatop found out from his spaceship's navigation system that the gateway to Baby Universe was not too far away. Unexpectedly, the spaceship computer announced the presence of an unidentified celestial body in front. Akatop commented that it was queer, as he had surveyed and logged everything in this part of the Galaxy during his last trip here. He checked with King Clone and Prince Energy and both said they had never seen this object before. So the group decided to take a closer look...

The space travellers were following the golden trail to Baby Universe when they came across an unidentified celestial object. From far away, it appeared to be a smooth, shiny, silvery ball-shaped object. The odd thing was that this object was not flying at a constant speed nor was it stationary. This object was actually moving in a very erratic way; forwards, sideways, backwards, then forwards again repeatedly. This could have only meant one thing for sure: whatever this object was, it was not a meteor or a planet. With the magnified view on the two spaceships' viewscreens, the travellers noticed that the ball was completely covered by some silvery matter. King Clone called the silvery matter the 'cloud', like the clouds on Earth. They could not tell what was underneath the 'cloud' even with the use of sophisticated spaceship radars. No one had ever seen anything like this before. Akatop said maybe it was an unknown alien spaceship in distress. He tried hailing the unknown object using the universal call signal but was unsuccessful.

The object showed no response.

The group surrounded this mysterious object, hoping to identify it or offer assistance if needed. The ball started its unpredictable chaotic moves again and everyone scrambled to avoid getting hit by it. A Firebird was in the wrong place at the wrong time and collided with the moving ball and promptly disappeared into the silvery 'cloud'. This unfortunate Firebird immediately sent out an SOS signal saying that he was totally stuck and couldn't move. Upon hearing his plea, two other Firebirds instantly dived in for the rescue. Alas, they also ended up with the same fate. Upon seeing this, Prince Energy immediately left King Clone's spaceship; he morphed into a fireball and shot straight into and burned away the part of the silvery 'cloud' that had entrapped the three Firebirds and freed them.

The ball-shaped object instantaneously woke up with the silvery 'cloud' changing from a smooth to a wavy appearance. Next, everyone saw numerous silvery threads shooting out towards them, followed by the emergence of large silvery spiders crawling up the silvery threads. The spiders started casting more and more silvery threads to make a huge spider web closing in on the space travellers, trying to entrap them.

Everyone had to move quickly. Princess Adventura and King Clone performed the emergency maneuvers and steered their spaceships out of harm's way. Dragon Prince and the Firebirds quickly flew away from the web to avoid getting entangled by it. The Firebirds shot fire at the web but their flames were not hot enough to melt the threads.

Prince Energy was the only one not bothered at all. He leisurely darted here and there and everywhere. Whenever his flame touched the web, the threads just melted away.

King Clone was powering up his spaceship's weapons to shoot down the spiders but he stopped after Princess Adventura persuaded him not to do so. Very quickly the silvery spiders realized that they were no match for the fiery fireball - Prince Energy - who was burning the spider web away faster than it was being formed. The silvery spiders retreated into the 'cloud' and stopped shooting out any more threads. Next, as a sign of truce or subordination or surrender, a circular opening appeared in the 'cloud' and the group perceived it as an invitation to go inside.

When they cautiously flew through the opening, the group found that the silvery 'cloud' was actually a very thick layer of spider threads completely surrounding a huge oval shaped object in the center. They saw a large number of silvery spiders clinging on threads hanging down from the 'cloud' layer towards this object. It had a beautiful, smooth, shiny, silvery, curved surface onto which everyone landed, including the two spaceships, Dragon Prince, the Firebirds and Prince Energy (who had morphed back into a human figure). Then everyone received a telepathic message, "Welcome to Silvery Spider Nest. I am Queen Spider." They all became entranced by a pair of strikingly beautiful eyes appearing from one far end of the surface. Fortunately, no one had arachnophobia, because they were all standing on the back of a huge silvery space spider.

Princess Adventura explained to the huge silvery queen spider that the group were space travellers passing by and meant no harm. They learned that Queen Spider and her colony were nomads roaming in space. They were actually harmless and beneficial entities that served as garbage collectors, trapping the space rocks, space debris and junk as their food. When the three Firebirds got entrapped and Prince Energy was burning the web, the spiders thought they were being invaded and were unsuccessfully putting up a defensive fight.

Akatop asked Queen Spider why the colony was moving in such an erratic pattern. After a slight hesitation, Queen Spider in a sad tone told the group that she was blind. This happened one day while she and her colony were roaming in space and she accidently faced a sun when a gargantuan solar flare occurred. She did not turn away fast enough and her eyes were damaged by the sun's radiation. The kindhearted Princess Adventura exclaimed, "Oh, I am sorry." Akatop explained that it was the light receptor cell units inside Queen Spider's eyes that were damaged by the solar radiation. The sympathetic princess asked Akatop if there was any way to restore Queen Spider's eyesight. Akatop replied that he did not think so.

Princess Adventura was adamant and kept asking questions, "What about eye transplant?"

Akatop said that was impossible because nobody had done it before on a giant spider. Princess Adventura would not give up. She asked about using medications to heal the eyes and received the negative reply that chemicals would not work. She proposed the use of nano computer chips for creating artificial eyes and the negative reply was that nobody knew how the giant spider eye worked. So back and forth the two debated until suddenly Akatop had an idea. Scratching his big head Akatop said, "Oh yes. Maybe I can try using the healing stone Bodhi gave me and see what happens."

Upon hearing this Princess Adventura excitedly said, "Quick, let's do it."

Akatop asked, "But how?"

They went over to Queen Spider's two beautiful main eyes that were staring at them with the tantalizing stare. Princess Adventura had the profound feeling of sympathy and sadness in knowing that these two most beautiful eyes were sightless. Akatop took the healing stone from the buckle of his belt and, while holding it in his right hand, contemplated what to do next. He and Princess Adventura were unprepared and surprised by what happened next. The stone suddenly radiated multi-coloured lights and abruptly flew from his hand into the crown part of Queen Spider's head. Everyone heard Queen Spider crying out loud in a joyful tone, "Oh, I can see!" A miracle had happened. Everyone cheered and the whole colony of silvery spiders went wild, running around spinning webs and more webs into space.

Queen Spider was very happy and she thanked Princess Adventura and Akatop profusely for restoring her eyesight. She also thanked Princess Adventura for her kind act of stopping the targeting of the silvery spiders by the spaceship weapons. Queen Spider presented two spindles of silvery spider threads as gratitude, one each to Princess Adventura and Akatop. After conferring with Akatop and King Clone, Princess Adventura invited the silvery spiders to become members of United Universes. Queen Spider gracefully accepted.

The meeting ended happily and the travellers resumed their journey after bidding goodbye to Queen Spider and her colony of silvery spiders. Upon leaving, they found out that the golden trail had disappeared. They were certain that the golden trail had purposely guided them to Queen Spider. In fact, the overlord of the new galaxy had heard Queen Spider's moans and cries and had felt her pain. The overlord had guided the space travellers to meet and cure Queen Spider's blindness.

After the spider encounter, the rest of the trip through the Galaxy was uneventful. Princess Adventura was becoming a seasoned space traveller and she appreciated more of the many wonders of the universe. The more supernatural phenomena and strange events she encountered, the less surprised she would feel and the more enthusiastic she became about the wonders and mysteries of space.

Under Akatop's guidance, Princess Adventura flew the spaceship smoothly through the gateway into Baby Universe. Once inside, they waited for the others to get across. When everyone was together again, Prince Energy contacted his parents, who were pleased to hear that their son and his friends were coming for a visit. King Time instructed the group to start flying towards the center of Baby Universe while he was going to create a wormhole and, once that was set up, the group could use it as a shortcut to reach Planet Royal. He said because Baby Universe had expanded much larger than the last time when Akatop and King Clone visited, it would take them a very long time to reach Planet Royal. Prince Energy told the rest of the group that since his parents would be busy for a while making the wormhole, he and the Firebirds would have a quick meeting with his younger brother, Prince Dark Energy, who was at the far end of Baby Universe.

After Prince Energy and the twelve Firebirds left, Akatop and King Clone programmed their spaceships to fly at maximum speed in autopilot mode towards the center of Baby Universe where Planet Royal was located. Dragon Prince flew effortlessly next to Akatop's spaceship. Everyone eagerly watched for the appearance of the wormhole. The bewildered Princess Adventura marveled at the complete darkness and the void feeling of this universe. She commented that there were no stars or celestial lights visible as far as she could see or detect using the spaceship's radar. Akatop explained that Baby Universe was at its infancy and the royal couple was still creating their kingdom.

All of a sudden a speck of light appeared out of nowhere and rapidly approached the two spaceships. It was not the wormhole. What could it be? The space travellers had run into another unforgettable and unimaginable encounter that almost ended tragically!

The space travellers were flying to the center of Baby Universe when they encountered another unexpected and scary event. They saw in the complete darkness of the vast Baby Universe a tiny speck of light suddenly appearing far away. The light was racing towards them so quickly that within a blink of an eye, it was in front of the two spaceships and Dragon Prince. The raindrop-sized light dot then instantly divided into three tiny dots. Each light dot chose its own target from among the two spaceships and Dragon Prince. The dots circled their targets once and then as if on cue all three converged simultaneously onto the outer surface of Akatop's spaceship. Behaving like patches of liquid mercury on the spaceship's hull surface, the three light dots spread and coalesced so rapidly that this unknown substance promptly covered up the whole spaceship.

While all this was happening, Princess Adventura's gold pendant and Akatop's magic belt began to emit a special multi-coloured light and created an impenetrable force field that enveloped the two adventurers.

Alas, the next scene was unimaginable but fascinating and shocking to watch. To everyone's horror, the big spaceship instantly vanished and in its place all the spaceship's structural components and parts drifted freely and chaotically. Wait, what happened to Princess Adventura and Akatop who were inside the spaceship? The two occupants were floating in space cocooned inside two bubbles of light force field. The liquid-like substance covered the bubbles up completely.

This unbelievable and terrifying event happened so fast that by the time King Clone and Dragon Prince wanted to react, all they saw were the two man-sized bubbles covered with the unknown substance stuck together and suspended in space. King Clone worried that if he destroyed the unknown substance using his spaceship's laser gun, the laser fire could kill his two friends at the same time.

Dragon Prince, having the special link with Princess Adventura, knew right away that she was safe inside the bubble light force field. Somehow Dragon Prince could also link with Akatop, who wore the magic belt from Bodhi, and found out that Akatop was all right too. Dragon Prince suddenly received instructions from an unknown source. Dragon Prince, who was made of stardust, used his special power to transform himself into a super powerful magnetic metallic dragon. He flew towards the mysterious substance, which promptly left the two bubbles and streamed rapidly towards the metallic dragon, coating him completely. When the mysterious substance moved to Dragon Prince, the two bubbles were freed. King Clone quickly maneuvered his spaceship to pick up his two friends in their light shield bubbles. When the two bubbles were inside the spaceship, the light force field vanished.

The whole commotion lasted only a few seconds and then it was over. After Princess Adventura and Akatop got on board, King Clone reset his spaceship back to maximum speed in autopilot mode and continued the journey to the center of Baby Universe. Dragon Prince flew leisurely and effortlessly at a safe distance from the spaceship. The unknown substance could not affect his magnetic and metallic form. However, he did not want his magnetic force to disrupt Fantastic Cloud's computers. Nobody had any clue what the unknown substance was. Although everyone felt bad about the loss of Akatop's spaceship, Akatop calmly said in his normal voice, "Let's hope the rest of our journey is smooth going."

Unfortunately, the trip was anything but uneventful and they quickly encountered another life threatening situation. Shortly after they had resumed their journey, Fantastic Cloud's onboard computer announced the warning that it had lost control of the spaceship. The three space travellers found that Fantastic Cloud had veered away from the programmed route and, together with Dragon Prince, they were flying at a velocity far above the spaceship's own maximum speed. Dragon Prince told them that they were being pulled by an invisible force so enormously powerful that even he could not overcome its pulling force. Almost immediately, Fantastic Cloud's long-range radar detected the presence of an object far away ahead of them. The spaceship and the dragon continued to accelerate and in no time they were rapidly approaching this space object. They knew then that the tremendously powerful force that was pulling the spaceship and Dragon Prince must have been coming from this object.

Akatop quickly used the spaceship computer to analyze the radar and sonar data and told the others that it was a spherical object about the size of the moon that orbited Earth. As the spaceship was closing in, Princess Adventura tried to get a visual image of the sphere on the spaceship's viewscreen but failed due to the total darkness of Baby Universe.

King Clone tried desperately to regain control of Fantastic Cloud but his attempts were futile. Dragon Prince could not free himself from the pulling force either. Unfortunately, as the still accelerating Fantastic Cloud and Dragon Prince flew towards the spherical object, the spaceship's computer blasted the alarm repeatedly 'Collision! Danger!' The doomed space travellers, with horrified looks and sickened feelings, prepared themselves for the inevitable collision.

To everyone's surprise, when Fantastic Cloud and Dragon Prince collided with the sphere, no one got hurt or killed. They just flew through a thick layer of unknown substance similar to the dense clouds on Earth. Once through the cloud, they were flying in open space hundreds of miles from a solid core that was about 1/10th the size of Earth's moon inside the sphere. It was déjà vu for both Akatop and King Clone who had had a similar experience while almost crash landing on Planet Medicina in Bubble Universe.

After they passed through the cloud layer, the space travellers found out that the tremendously powerful pulling force, although weakened, was still strong enough to pull Fantastic Cloud and Dragon Prince towards the sphere's solid core. King Clone had to keep the spaceship at maximum power output just to fly at a fixed circular orbit to prevent it from being pulled to the solid core. Dragon Prince had to flap his wings at fixed intervals to avoid being pulled all the way to the solid core. They could not free themselves and ended up just flying around and around the solid core at a safe and fixed orbit.

After the first orbit, Akatop had enough surveillance data from the spaceship radar and sonar to declare that -

1/ the solid core had a very ragged surface making landing the spaceship on it impossible

2/ the solid core was 100% solid made by fusion of the space rocks and debris and other unknown materials

3/ Fantastic Cloud's weapons were not powerful enough to break the core apart

4/ Akatop postulated that the pulling force was radiating from the solid core and that the cloud layer magnified the force many times

5/ eventually, everyone onboard would be killed when Fantastic Cloud ran out of fuel and collided with the solid core

6/ Dragon Prince would be flying around the solid core forever, unable to escape the pulling force.

Those were depressing news for everyone; the three space travellers and Dragon Prince were doomed for sure.

Fortunately they were all saved by a miracle.

Inside the mysterious spherical object, the spaceship and Dragon Prince maintained their fixed and safe orbits flying around the solid core for some time. To the space travellers it felt like an eternity. Suddenly a miracle happened. King Time's majestic face materialized in front of the spaceship and Dragon Prince. Everyone heard a benevolent voice saying, "There you are. I have been looking for you and was worried that you were lost on the way." King Time said that the wormhole to Planet Royal was ready for the space travellers to fly through. With a very gentle puff, King Time blew Fantastic Cloud and Dragon Prince away from the solid core through the cloud layer of the spherical object out to space where the wormhole was already waiting for them. King Clone hastily flew Fantastic Cloud followed by Dragon Prince into the wormhole to Planet Royal, bypassing its protective asteroid belts.

They arrived at Planet Royal very quickly. At the royal palace, the royal couple, along with Prince Energy and the twelve Firebirds who had arrived earlier, met with the latecomers: golden coloured King Clone, Princess Adventura dressed in a combat jumpsuit, metallic Dragon Prince, and Akatop without his spaceship.

Immediately after the greeting, the royal couple said that they already knew the purpose of the group's visit. King Time told Princess Adventura not to worry because her planet was safe and sound. Upon hearing the good news, Princess Adventura's body glow turned brighter and a big smile appeared on her face. King Time had already informed the twelve Firebirds who had arrived earlier that their planet was OK. King Time said that he would explain more about what happened to the two missing planets during lunch.

Prince Energy asked how it was possible that he had only left the group momentarily and Akatop lost his spaceship and Dragon Prince turned into a metallic dragon. After Akatop told Prince Energy what had happened, King Time waved his hand and behold, a large screen appeared next to him and everyone saw on screen millions and millions of tiny stationary robots covering the metallic dragon.

King Time said a young overlord of a new galaxy had been to Planet Royal to see the royal couple before the group came to visit. On leaving Planet Royal, the overlord inadvertently left behind his toy - the nano robots that had been roaming harmlessly inside Baby Universe afterwards. One of the nano robots' functions, metal assimilation, was somehow accidently turned on. The nano robots would assimilate and convert any metal they came into contact with, and use all the converted metal molecules to replicate more nano robots to the nth order. The nano robots were extremely sophisticated and efficient machines so that within a few nanoseconds there could be an astronomical number of nano robots. The nano robots would not convert any non-metallic objects.

When the group entered Baby Universe, the nano robots had detected and found the spaceships, resulting in the commotion. After Akatop's spaceship was assimilated, the metallic parts of the communicator Akatop was carrying and the platinum medals and bracelet Princess Adventura was wearing attracted the nano robots and they converged on the bubbles enclosing Akatop and Princess Adventura. Fortunately, the special light force field bubbles protected them from getting asphyxiated in space.

King Time explained that King Clone's spaceship was coated with the golden rays of golden phoenix that was the overlord's personal ride. The overlord was the master of the nano robots, and so the robots did not assimilate King Clone's spaceship. King Time said to Dragon Prince, "You were instructed by Bodhi to metallize and magnetize. Turning yourself into metal made the nano robots attach to your body and at the same time the magnetic field deactivated them so that you were not assimilated. You can now change back to your true form because I have re-programmed the nano robots to be under your command temporarily until they are returned to their master, the overlord." Right away the metallic dragon became the magnificent green Dragon Prince again with a sparkling silvery pea-sized sphere, the colony of nano robots, resting on the top of his head.

King Time continued, "A young bubble planet had accidentally wandered from Bubble Universe into Baby Universe some time ago. The bubble planet was pulling in any space objects in its vicinity to become part of its solid core so it could grow. Somehow the bubble planet happened to be in that part of Baby Universe where King Clone's spaceship and Dragon Prince were and entrapped them".

After King Time finished talking, Prince Energy said he wanted to take Dragon Prince and the twelve Firebirds around for a tour of Planet Royal and they zoomed into the sky and disappeared. Princess Adventura, this being her first time to the royal palace, was awed by and marveled at its majestic decor and heavenly grand ornaments. The royal couple took Princess Adventura, Akatop and King Clone to the dining hall. During the luncheon, King Time told the three what had happened to the missing Planet Imaginata.

King Time said, "Whenever a new galaxy is formed, an overlord will be born to become its keeper. For a limited time right after the overlord becomes the gatekeeper, he must pay a visit to the overlords of other galaxies in different universes. During his tour, the new overlord is granted special powers for him to transport any planets or stars he chooses from other galaxies to his own galaxy. There is only one strict criterion: the chosen planet or star must be deemed to be in trouble, for example, about to be swallowed by an approaching black hole; at danger of being damaged from collision with an asteroid; the planet's occupants are going to be destroyed; and other such reasons.

The overlord who visited us earlier was from the new galaxy formed by the merger of two galaxies, the same ones Prince Energy and the Firebirds went to observe in space. This overlord had informed us that he had transported Planet Imaginata to his galaxy after he foresaw that in the very near future a black hole would suddenly show up in Planet Imaginata's neighborhood and consume the planet. Other than the change of location to a new galaxy, everything remained the same on the moved planet afterwards."

By this time, Prince Energy, Dragon Prince and the twelve Firebirds had returned from their tour and they joined the party. Glancing at the twelve Firebirds, King Time resumed his speech, "The overlord also transported the dying Planet of Firebirds to his galaxy. The Firebirds had been away from their planet too long. Because of their neglect, the fires on the planet were petering out and the fire worms were dying. The overlord relocated the planet to orbit a flaming star at the right distance to temporarily rekindle the fires and save the fire worms. The overlord has recommended that the Firebirds return more often and take better care of their planet."

Everyone saw a holographic 3-D star map materializing at the center of the dining hall. Queen Space pointed at the location of the new galaxy. She said, "After leaving Baby Universe, you will have to fly through a small universe to reach the new galaxy. I have to forewarn you with the caveat that you need to be very cautious because this universe has a very hostile environment. There are interplanetary skirmishes going on among the warring planets; deadly swarms of space locusts; and showers of asteroids and meteors. Be extra careful. Prince Energy, please do what you can to help."

Everyone had a fabulous luncheon. Afterwards, upon leaving the dining hall, the royal couple led the group to a hallway that had many holographic pictures on one wall. The visitors were dumbfounded by what they saw. Princess Adventura saw her Planet Imaginata in a new galaxy. When she moved closer to have a better look, the picture switched to a close up view and she saw Imaginatans happily going about doing their usual daily activities at the city square. Then she saw her parents entertaining some guests inside the palace. King Clone saw his own royal family and some of his people living joyfully on the giant tree of Planet Strange. Akatop was astonished to see that his fellow scientists on his home planet were constructing a new spaceship with his name painted on the hull, as if they knew he had lost his spaceship. The twelve Firebirds saw the fire worms laying eggs on the surface of their planet.

Queen Space said to the visitors, "The holographic scenes show what you want to see which is real life happening in real time on your planets." Princess Adventura then fully appreciated what King Time meant when he said nothing was changed on the moved planet.

The grateful visitors thanked the royal couple for providing them with these heartwarming and homecoming experiences. By then, Princess Adventura was getting a bit homesick. As if to comfort her, motherly Queen Space waved her hand and suddenly the princess found that she was dressed in a beautiful hooded silvery jumpsuit. Queen Space explained that she used some of Princess Adventura's space spider thread to make the jumpsuit. She laughingly said she would be the first one in space who knew how to make clothes with the space spider's thread. She told Princess Adventura that space spider thread was one of the most precious materials in the universe. The space spider thread was virtually indestructible and only Celestial Fire could melt it, and the thread could stretch to unimaginable length. By wearing the space spider thread jumpsuit, the princess would be thermally insulated against extremely hot and cold temperatures. Princess Adventura was ecstatic on hearing this and she thanked Queen Space for the beautiful jumpsuit.

At the same time, King Time was saying that if King Clone fanned the golden feather to enlarge it to the size of a surfboard, he could surf on the golden feather to anywhere in space. King Time also said that because the golden rays of the hatching golden phoenix egg coated King Clone, no fire could hurt him. On hearing this, King Clone was overjoyed as all his life he was afraid of being burnt by fire! He thanked King Time for telling him such good news.

By this time, everyone was preparing to leave. With King Time's permission, Akatop went to the royal library and downloaded a copy of the relevant star map of the hostile universe and the new galaxy onto King Clone's spaceship computer. Akatop and King Clone had promised Princess Adventura that they would accompany her for her reunification with her family and her people on Planet Imaginata. Of course, Dragon Prince would be going as well. The rest of the party consisted of the twelve Firebirds and Prince Energy who told his parents he wanted to explore the new galaxy. Before leaving Planet Royal, Dragon Prince contacted his one hundred and seven fellow dragons who were searching all over space looking for the missing Planet Imaginata. The dragons said they would rejoin their leader as quickly as possible.

Because Baby Universe was so vast and still expanding, King Time said he would create another new wormhole for the travellers to use as a shortcut to the next universe. So, very soon afterwards, the travellers were on their way. The first one to fly into King Time's wormhole was King Clone. He happily stood on his golden feather surfboard, forgetting all about Queen Space's warning that when they exited the wormhole it would be very hazardous. Next to him was Prince Energy in the form of a fireball followed by the twelve Firebirds. Close behind was Akatop and Princess Adventura copiloting Fantastic Cloud; and Dragon Prince flying next to the spaceship.

The trip through the wormhole was quick and smooth. When they exited at the other end of the wormhole, the space travellers entered the hostile universe. Immediately they found themselves in a very dire situation and had to try their hardest to avoid getting injured or killed.

Chapter 10 – Journey through Hostile Universe

Following King Time's instructions, the space travellers flew through the new wormhole to enter the hostile universe located between Baby Universe and the new galaxy. The advantage of using the wormhole was that the group saved time and distance, bypassing most of Baby Universe. The huge drawback of the new wormhole was that even its creator King Time could not know beforehand what awaited the space travellers when they exited the wormhole.

The space travellers found out that they were paying a great price for taking the shortcut. Upon exiting the wormhole, they flew straight into the middle of a massive meteoroid shower.

Princess Adventura, who was copiloting Fantastic Cloud, saw close to one hundred meteoroids ranging from 10 meters in diameter to golf ball size, all shooting towards the group. The inexperienced Princess Adventura hesitated slightly. Akatop calmly stepped in and took over full control of the spaceship. He instantly switched on the spaceship's weapon system to shoot lasers at the larger meteoroids, breaking them apart. He skillfully piloted the spaceship to perform evasive maneuvers. But there were just too many meteoroids and Fantastic Cloud still got hit by some of the small sized ones. If a large one collided with the spaceship, it would be damaged, putting Princess Adventura and Akatop in danger.

The situation was getting precarious. King Clone was batting the smaller meteoroids away with his magic staff and sidestepping the larger ones. At the front of the group, Prince Energy just blasted his way through. When Prince Energy saw the spaceship having a hard time with the incoming space rocks, he immediately moved to position himself ahead of Fantastic Cloud and helped destroy some meteoroids. When King Clone saw that, he morphed into a giant King Clone and his feather transformed into a giant surfboard. He then got in front of Fantastic Cloud. With the two helping, no more space rocks could hit the spaceship. Meanwhile, Dragon Prince and the Firebirds were performing evasive maneuvers to avoid the dangerous incoming flying objects.

The meteoroids flew by quickly and space became silent and empty again. Apart from several Firebirds having bruised wings, no one was seriously hurt. King Clone and his feather reverted to normal size. After regrouping, the space travellers continued on with their journey.

Since nobody had been to this universe before, they had no clue as to where they were. Working with the hypothesis that they were in the sector of the hostile universe closest to Baby Universe, Akatop plotted the best-estimate route to the new galaxy for them. Fantastic Cloud led the way with the rest following behind. Akatop told the others, "According to the map from King Time's library, this universe is very small, about the size of solar system of my universe. I anticipate that very soon we will fly by a landmark, two small planets close to each other."

Upon hearing his remarks, everyone was on the lookout for the planets. Princess Adventura remarked that this universe was quite bright as she could easily see Dragon Prince and the Firebirds flying next to the spaceship. She asked the all-knowing Akatop why and he replied that there must have been a sun close to them somewhere inside this universe.

Just as they were talking, the spaceship's long-range radar detected the presence of celestial objects far away. Akatop requested Princess Adventura, who was piloting the spaceship, to steer towards the objects so they could have a better look. Everyone followed the spaceship to the unknown objects. When they were close enough, the spaceship's forward viewscreen revealed the image of two planets. Akatop calculated the distance between these two moon-sized planets was likely equaled to 1/3rd of that from Earth to moon, so these two planets were very close to each other indeed. He told the others, "With this landmark I know exactly where we are now. To save time let's just fly by the planets without stopping."

Everyone agreed.

Unfortunately, events did not unfold as planned because something happened that made them change their plans.

Akatop had asked Princess Adventura to fly Fantastic Cloud through space midway between the two planets instead of landing on one of them. Just as the group was flying through, something unexpectedly happened. The spaceship's computer sounded the alarm repeatedly, "Danger, multiple incoming projectiles." Indeed, the spaceship's radar detected many fast moving objects, and on the viewscreen there were missiles coming at them. Akatop quickly alerted the others to take evasive action. It turned out the missiles were not aimed at them at all. The two planets were firing missiles at each other and the group just happened to be in the way of the missile flight paths. The missiles just went by the group and then exploded on contact with the targeted planets. Then another missile salvo came, followed by another salvo again.

Dragon Prince was really upset when he saw the vast numbers of flying missiles. He commanded the nano robots to assimilate all the deadly arsenals. Within a very short time, the missiles all vanished after the nano robots assimilated them. Princess Adventura said that it was not right for the two neighboring planets to be at war and she wanted to find out why. Akatop asked King Clone to come inside Fantastic Cloud and together the three ambassadors of United Universes would visit the two warring planets. He suggested that Prince Energy, Dragon Prince and the Firebirds could wait in space until the three returned. Everyone agreed.

So the three ambassadors flew to one of the planets.

They were bewildered by what they saw on the planet. It was a smaller version of Earth with similar weather, landscape and atmosphere. The occupants on this planet appeared to have the same physical appearance as the human race on Earth. Everyone was wearing blue clothes! At first, the occupants, who spoke a human language, were scared by the appearance from the sky of a talking monkey, a tall glowing female human-like creature, and a queer-looking alien. But once the planet's occupants found out that the three alien visitors could speak their language, their fear dissipated immediately.

The three alien visitors were escorted to see the commander-in-chief, Victo. The three introduced themselves as ambassadors of United Universes and were welcomed warmly. Over the next few minutes, they found out why the two planets were at war with each other; the two groups of people had depleted the natural resources of their respective planets. The residents of each planet were trying to conquer and take over the other planet. Fortunately, the people of these two planets were anti-nuclear and they were using conventional weapons only.

On hearing this from Victo, Akatop said that he might be able to help if he could find out a bit more about the planet's difficulty with its natural resources. With Victo's consent, Akatop did a quick analysis of the planet's library computer memory data and discovered that this race was many hundred Earth years behind the humans on Earth in the fields of computer science and other technologies! Akatop noticed that this planet was energy dependent on fossil fuels that were rapidly depleting.

Akatop then asked Victo and the other leaders, "Will you stop fighting each other if we teach you how to be energy efficient and how to manufacture things easily?"

Victo and his countrymen replied that they would stop the war right away if the opposite party agreed to stop fighting as well. Akatop recommended to Victo that he should videoconference with the leader of the other planet to convey the proposal and message. Victo immediately called his counterpart, Successo, who gave an affirmative reply. A truce was arranged right after the conference call. Akatop then asked if King Clone would give away a couple of 3-D printing machines from Fantastic Cloud.

King Clone said, "No problem, go ahead." Akatop took one machine and demonstrated how it worked and gave it with the blue print to Victo's engineers who were amazed at this miracle equipment. Akatop taught the engineers how to use hydrogen as a clean energy source, just like when he and his people taught the humans on Earth the same technology in the past.

The three ambassadors flew to the other planet to meet Successo. Other than wearing red clothes, the people on the second planet were no different than Victo's people on the first planet. Successo's people were all happy when Akatop repeated the same feat in giving them a 3-D printing machine with its blueprint and hydrogen technology. The people of these two planets were overjoyed that they would no longer have to fight each other.

Afterwards, Princess Advantura officially invited the two planets to become members of United Universes and the two leaders and their congresses heartily accepted the invitation. It was a miracle that the three ambassadors achieved all these within half a day's time. King Clone jokingly told Akatop that he was the best negotiator and mediator in the universe. Princess Adventura also agreed and said that she had learned a lot of negotiation skills. They flew back to space and rejoined and thanked Prince Energy, Dragon Prince, and the Firebirds who were patiently waiting for the three.

Without further delay, the group restarted their journey with the spaceship leading the way. Akatop said that it would not take long for them to fly through the rest of this universe and enter the new galaxy. King Clone said that he would pilot Fantastic Cloud so that Akatop and Princess Adventura could take a break. Prince Energy, the dragon, and the Firebirds of course did not need to rest at all.

Just when everyone thought it would be smooth and easygoing the rest of the trip, the spaceship's radar announced the presence of a thick layer of unknown materials in front. King Clone thought it was some cosmic dust and wasn't worried at first until the spaceship computer started sounding the alarm repeatedly, "Intruder alert! Intruder alert!" Simultaneously, King Clone heard repeatedly thumping noises originating from the hull of Fantastic Cloud. Akatop and Princess Adventura were also alerted and came back to the command center from the small lounge of the spaceship. They saw on the viewscreen innumerous flying darts coming at them.

When Princess Adventura saw the magnified view of the darts, she exclaimed, "Locust swarm!" She remembered reading about it in her biology class in school. King Clone commented that these space locusts were about five times the size of the ones on Earth. There must have been thousands upon thousands of the space critters surrounding the group.

Some distance ahead of the spaceship, Prince Energy was burning his way out of the space locust swarm, trying to clear a pathway for the spaceship. The space locusts largely avoided the twelve flaming Firebirds. Dragon Prince appeared to have some troubles. Flapping his huge wings, he was selflessly trying to protect the spaceship; forgetting about himself, he was swamped by the space locusts. Fantastic Cloud was completely covered by layers and layers of the space critters. King Clone had to shut down the spaceship's engines to prevent the insects from being sucked into the engines and causing damage.

If this continued, they would all die when the space locusts overwhelmed them.

Ah, here came the rescue. In space, out of the blue, came the returning one hundred and seven dragons; they had caught up with their leader Dragon Prince and found him and his friends in distress. After forming a circle around the tired and overwhelmed group, the newly arrived dragons flapped their huge and powerful wings to blow away the incoming space insects, thus preventing them from swarming Dragon Prince and Fantastic Cloud. Prince Energy and the twelve Firebirds continued to burn the incoming space locusts. Waves and waves of space locusts just kept coming for a while, making the reinforcing dragons feel the pressure too. Eventually, the swarm of space locusts passed the group.

Everyone was all right.

Fantastic Cloud was now a greyish brown colour with layers of space locusts covering the hull. Dragon Prince and a couple of flying dragons gently blew away the space locusts from Fantastic Cloud's hull to return it to the beautiful golden colour. Afterwards, the group continued their flight through the universe quickly and smoothly. They flew through the gateway to the new galaxy. The moment the group entered the new galaxy the sphere of nano robots resting on Dragon Prince's head flew away immediately.

This new galaxy was unlike any other galaxy.

Even the most seasoned space travellers of the group, Akatop, Prince Energy and the twelve Firebirds, agreed that they had never seen a galaxy like this before. The space was softly lighted and warm; King Clone commented that it was like the clear sunset sky on Earth. Everyone felt comfortable and relaxed.

King Clone asked Princess Adventura to pilot Fantastic Cloud and then he jumped out of the spaceship onto his golden feather surfboard and happily zoomed around in space. Initially, Princess Adventura located a space object on the spaceship's radar and the group decided to fly over to have a look. From a distance, they saw a planet that was glowing on and off. Thinking that it was the missing Planet Imaginata, Princess Adventura got excited and her body glowed again.

However, when they flew close enough they found out that it was not Planet Imaginata but a planet with twelve glowing spherical entities on its surface. Each entity glowed intermittently in its own colour. The twelve spheres were of various sizes, the largest one three times the size of Dragon Prince to the smallest one that was two feet in diameter. The twelve spheres shot out of the surface of the planet fifty feet apart, the largest one first followed by the others in order of decreasing size. They followed the same semicircular projectile path, reaching high above the surface of the planet and then falling back to the planet. When they were above the planet surface, their unbelievable intense glow was easily seen in nearby space. The whole process repeated itself non-stop.

Awed but disappointed that this was not Planet Imaginata, the group resumed their search for the missing planets. Unfortunately, they did not really know how or where to look. The flying dragons wanted to help. So it was decided the main search group would be Princess Adventura and Akatop flying in Fantastic Cloud, with Dragon Prince next to it and the twelve Firebirds together with Prince Energy, the group's leader and protector. King Clone and the rest of the flying dragons would individually search the new galaxy.

King Clone said, "Let's go." Surfing on his golden feather King Clone and the one hundred and seven flying dragons and the main group were just about to disperse in one hundred and nine different directions into the new galaxy. They stopped abruptly when a beautiful golden flower that had never existed before appeared in the sector of space ahead, dazzling with multi-coloured light beams.

And then everyone saw the overlord.

The group saw the overlord of this new galaxy. He was in fact the young golden man riding the golden phoenix that they had seen earlier. On top of his head was the glowing planet flashing the multi-coloured lights. His facial profile was clearly visible, revealing his majestic appearance. The rest of him was in the form of a golden silhouette. The overlord was wearing King Clone's boots! He was riding on the golden phoenix that stood on the golden flower with its wings spread. The sphere of nano robots was floating above the golden phoenix's head.

Overlord Sanzin said to King Clone, "Thank you very much for your boots. I like them very much."

King Clone innocently replied, "Oh, the boots were a gift from Bodhi!"

Right then, a smiling Bodhi appeared next to Overlord Sanzin. Looking down at the three ambassadors of United Universes and Dragon Prince, Bodhi said, "Hello my friends, you surely had an exciting journey coming here." Everyone was overjoyed to see Bodhi again for it was a long time since they had parted ways.

Bodhi disappeared.

Overlord Sanzin continued to speak, "When I became overlord of this galaxy, I found out that I had an imperfect heart. Unless my heart gets repaired, very soon I shall be gone. This galaxy will not be able to survive on its own yet. All the planets in it will vanish before their time. The only way my heart can be repaired is to patch it with the gold heart pendant that Princess Adventura is wearing." The overlord paused and was just about to speak again.

Princess Adventura interrupted by saying eagerly that she would give Overlord Sanzin her gold heart pendant. She asked the overlord what she needed to do for the repair. A heart with a hole appeared in the silhouette of Overlord Sanzin. The overlord disappeared and the heart with the hole got bigger. Princess Adventura heard Overlord Sanzin's voice saying that dropping the pendant from the spaceship would not work. She had to personally put the gold heart pendant into the hole of the heart. However the caveat was that she would most probably die when she did it.

Princess Adventura replied that she would do it. She knew she would die but she also knew that her death would mean saving her family, her people on Planet Imaginata and all the other planets and their occupants in this galaxy. Princess Adventura was such a noble person that she would sacrifice herself for the good of many.

On hearing this, Dragon Prince, understanding fully and accepting that he would be killed at the same time as Princess Adventura, insisted that he would fly Princess Adventura through the hole of Overlord Sanzin's defective heart for the repair. True love between the two, they looked at each other, their eyes met and they smiled at each other.

Akatop and King Clone and the one hundred and seven flying dragons knew that there was nothing they could do to help. They solemnly watched Princess Adventura leaving Fantastic Cloud and getting onto the back of the waiting Dragon Prince. They felt very sad to see Princess Adventura and Dragon Prince taking their courageous and final death flight. The two zoomed into space straight into the hole of Overlord Sanzin's heart.

What happened next was the most unforgettable, unbelievable and magnificent phenomenon. When Princess Adventura and Dragon Prince disappeared inside the hole of Overlord Sanzin's heart, the hole closed up immediately and the heart started radiating soft and pure pink light that shone through space onto everything and every part of Sanzin Galaxy. When touched by the pink light, everyone felt good, happy and peaceful. The pink light lasted a blink of the eye and was gone and the heart disappeared at the same time. Knowing that Overlord Sanzin's heart was healed and Princess

Adventura and Dragon Prince were in a better place, Akatop and King Clone flew to Planet Imaginata to inform King Imak and Queen Gimma of their daughter's honourable self-sacrificing act. The royal couple was sad but proud of what their daughter did. Afterwards, Akatop and King Clone left for Planet Bacalona in Fantastic Cloud. The one hundred and seven flying dragons also left for their space exploration thinking that they had lost their leader.

What happened to Princess Adventura and Dragon Prince?

The moment they flew into the hole of Overlord Sanzin's heart they found themselves being whirled around violently as if they were picked up by a super powerful tornado. The rotating force was so strong that Princess Adventura was lifted off Dragon Prince's back and the two were separated from each other. She tried to grasp at the dragon but the formidable current kept pulling them further apart. Then she lost consciousness.

When she woke up, Princess Adventura found herself in a serene surrounding of the most comfortable pure white light and total silence. Princess Adventura ran around anxiously, desperately looking for the dragon. Then she saw him, Prince Nogard, instead of Dragon Prince. Prince Nogard saw her. They ran towards each other. Happily holding hands with each other, they felt the mutual indescribable feelings of love, joy, peace, kindness and wellness. The two must have been in heaven. They found out that there were stars and planets around them. With Prince Nogard morphing back into Dragon Prince and Princess Adventura riding on him the two would explore space and enjoy the moment. Other times Dragon Prince would change back to Prince Nogard and the two would walk hand-in-hand.

Sometime later, Overlord Sanzin, riding on the golden phoenix, appeared in front of them. He thanked Princess Adventura and Prince Nogard for healing his defective heart. Overlord Sanzin told them that they were on a heavenly planet in a galaxy inside his heart. They could explore space and enjoy their adventures in this new dimension. Overlord Sanzin said that in time when he became more powerful, he would be able to send the couple back to Planet Imaginata if they wished. He then vanished.

One Imaginatan year later, Akatop and King Clone were back on Planet Imaginata as guests of honour for the official opening of the memorial park of Princess Adventura. Prince Energy was also with them. The twelve Firebirds and the one hundred and seven flying dragons were circling in the sky above the park.

At the ceremony, King Imak and Queen Gimma unveiled Saviour of Planet Imaginata, a beautiful bronze statue of Princess Adventura riding on the back of a magnificent dragon, in front of all the guests and the dignitaries of Planet Imaginata. At that moment, from the sky above the statue, golden raindrops came down and coated the statue with a bright golden colour. Everyone on Planet Imaginata saw the golden silhouette of Overlord Sanzin riding on the golden phoenix in the sky. Then everyone saw the holographic view of a happy Princess Adventura with a big smile on her face riding on the back of a green dragon.

Princess Adventura waved and said, "Hello Mom and Dad, hello everybody, I'll be coming home soon."

END

Made in the USA
Charleston, SC
03 March 2015